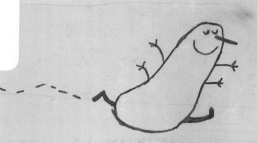

For Margot.
MM

For my family, my friends
and for Eunice.
DD

ORCHARD BOOKS
96 Leonard Street, London EC2A 4XD
Orchard Books Australia
Unit 31/56 O'Riordan Street, Alexandria, NSW 2015
First published in Great Britain in 2001
ISBN 1 84121 409 4
Text © Miriam Moss 2001
Illustrations © Delphine Durand 2001
The rights of Miriam Moss to be identified as the author and Delphine
Durand to be identified as the illustrator have been asserted by them
in accordance with the Copyright, Designs and Patents Act, 1988.
A CIP catalogue record for this book is available from the British Library
10 9 8 7 6 5 4 3 2 1
Printed in Singapore

Scritch Scratch

written by
Miriam Moss

pictures by
Delphine Durand

ORCHARD BOOKS

One day
a tiny insect,
no bigger than a small freckle,
climbed into Miss Calypso's classroom.

Nobody noticed...

Miss Calypso went on calling the register.
Ruby undid Polly's plait.
Joshua drew on Winston's back.
And Simon trimmed Karim's fringe.

The little louse had no wings.
But she had six strong legs
and she climbed straight into the Spelling Ship
hanging above Miss Calypso's head.

What a wonderful view!
Miss Calypso's cascading curls,
short crops, matted mops, tufty tops,
plaits, pigtails, ponytails...
even a frizzy wig on the plastic skeleton in the corner!

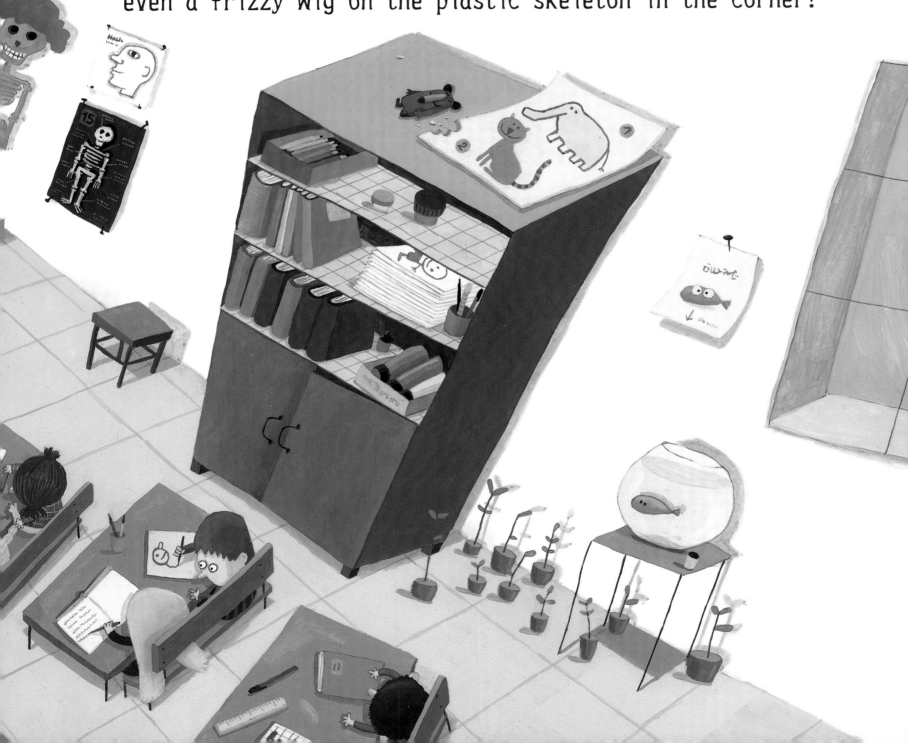

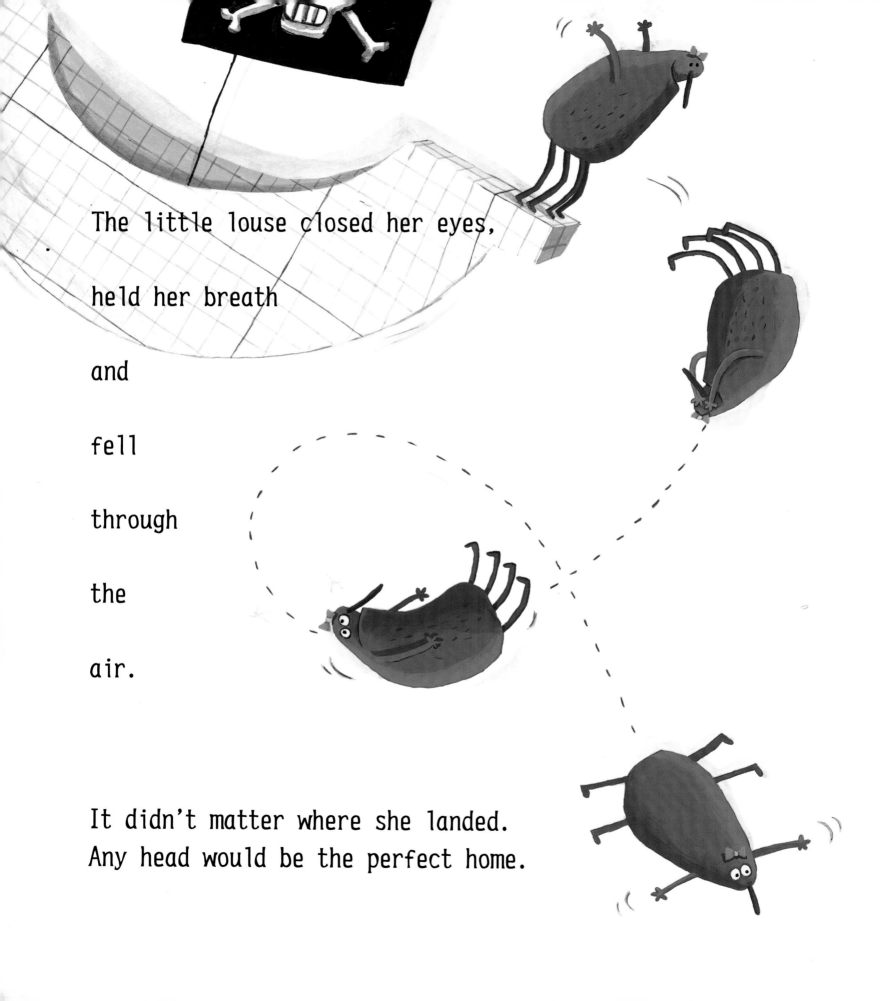

The little louse closed her eyes,

held her breath

and

fell

through

the

air.

It didn't matter where she landed.
Any head would be the perfect home.

And the perfect home she landed on was...

Miss Calypso!
The little louse got to work straight away,
sticking one tiny white egg to each
hair on Miss Calypso's head.

She hummed a happy tune.

Oh... No one knows from where I came,
A nit, a nibbler with no name,
But watch the teacher scritch and scratch,
When my creepy crawly family hatch.

Before long the creepy crawly family did hatch.
And they climbed into Miss Calypso's cascading curls.

Scritch Scratch went Miss Calypso,
                    praising Polly's pirate picture.

Scamper Scamper went the tiny headlice,
                    dancing down Polly's plait.

From
then on,
whenever
two
heads
touched,
lots of
little
headlice
moved
home!

Scritch Scratch went Polly,
playing with Ruby's hair.

Scamper Scamper went the headlice.

Scritch Scratch went Joshua,
drawing on Winston's back.

Scamper Scamper went the headlice.

Scritch Scratch went Simon,
trimming Karim's fringe.

Scamper Scamper went the headlice.

In no time at all,
the little lice had perfect homes
of their very own...

and that was when Mr Trout the Headmaster strode in!
"May I have a word, Miss Calypso?" he asked.
Miss Calypso agreed to meet him in the lunch hour
to discuss the scritching problem.

That night Mr Trout sent letters home to all the parents.

Dear Parents,
Please comb special conditioner through your children's hair and make it so slippery that all the headlice slide into the bathwater and float away

The next day the conditioned and combed
children returned to school.
There was not a single louse in sight.
They had all gone.

Well,
all
except
one!

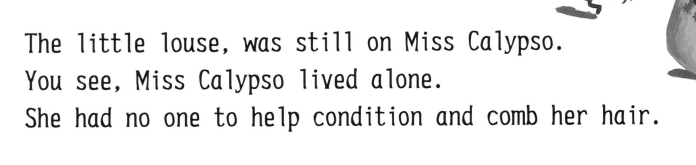

The little louse, was still on Miss Calypso.
You see, Miss Calypso lived alone.
She had no one to help condition and comb her hair.

Oh...

(hummed the little louse, who was now a grandmother)

No one knows from where we came,
We nits, we nibblers with no name,
Watch the children scritch and scratch,
When more creepy crawly families hatch.

Scritch Scratch went Miss Calypso.

Scamper Scamper went the headlice.

And soon the whole class was
scritching and scratching all over again!

Once again Mr Trout went to see Miss Calypso.
And there, in the little room where cups of tea
are made, Mr Trout found himself offering to
wash Miss Calypso's hair for her.

That night, while Mr Trout conditioned and combed Miss Calypso's hair, they fell in love. He fell in love with her cascading curls and she fell in love with his moustache.

So Mr Trout and Miss Calypso got married.
And now if you look into Mrs Trout's classroom—
what do you see?
Mrs Trout still calls the register.
Ruby still undoes Polly's plait.
Joshua still draws on Winston's back.
And Simon still trims Karim's fringe.

There's not a scritch or a scratch to be heard.
But...

there is a faint hum
from the classroom next door!

Oh... No one knows from where I came,
A nit, a nibbler with no name,
But watch the teacher scritch and scratch,
When my creepy crawly family hatch...